Erotic Collection 9

C J EDWARDS

ACKNOWLEDGMENTS

COVER DESIGN BY FRANCESSCA'S ROMANCE REVIEWS.
PROOFREADING BY KELSEY BURNS

CONTENTS

THE SPANKING DOCTOR.

Does your wife need a spanking? Are you a wife who is gagging to have her bottom reddened? Are you confused about domestic discipline? Stop worrying and call the spanking doctor.

"What do you think?" Dave turned the screen around and showed the ad to his twenty eight year old girlfriend of two years; Melanie.

"I think it would get me to pick the phone up," Mel grinned.

"As long as you put your phone number on the end that is!"

Forty year old Dave grinned back. "Less of your lip, young lady, or it'll be you that's squirming on my lap."

They shared a warm and knowing glance. That would hardly be anything new. Dave gave his young lady a good spanking on at least a weekly basis. It was what had brought them together and what gave them a solid bond that allowed them to play with other people, both together and separately without any fear for their relationship.

Up to now, spanking had been something personal they had kept to themselves. This was now about to change. Dave was keen to see if the intense feelings he got when disciplining a woman could be replicated on a casual basis and Melanie couldn't wait to see another helpless woman wriggling under Dave's strong arm; not to mention being watched herself.

It took all of two hours after posting the ad to a couple of suitable websites for Dave's mobile to ring. "Hello," said a male voice, "I'm phoning about your post on Spanking for Pleasure."

"Hello," said Dave. "Are you phoning for your wife or girlfriend?"

"My wife, Angela."

"Is she there?"

"She's right next to me."

"Okay," said Dave. "Put her on the phone."

"Hello," a timid female voice said almost immediately."

"I'm Master David," Dave replied. You will address me that way when you speak to me. Are you Angela?"

"Yes Master David," Angela replied.

Not one to beat around the bush, Dave jumped straight in. "Why do you want your bottom spanked Angela?"

There was a pause while the woman thought about that. "Erm, I do a job where I'm bossy all day and sometimes I feel I just want somebody to tell me what to do and sort of take me in hand. Is that all right?" she added hopefully.

"That's very honest of you, Angela. What is your job?"
I'm a maths teacher."

"I see!" Dave paused for effect. "How would you describe yourself Angela? Physically I mean. Will I find you attractive?"

"Well, I'm five foot nine, with light brown hair that goes to my shoulders. I'm told my face is pretty; I have large brown eyes and pouty lips…"

"What are your measurements, Angela?"

"36C-24-34."

"Very nice. Describe your nipples. Do they stick through your clothes when you're cold or excited?"

"Yes, they are very obvious."

"Do other men find you attractive?"

"Yes."

"How do you know?"

"I often catch them looking at me when they think I haven't noticed."

"Good. Are they sexually excited?"

"Sometimes!"

"So you look straight back at their cocks! What about other women?"

"Excuse me…Master David?"

"Do you catch other women looking at you?"

Angela paused and was clearly embarrassed when she answered in a low voice. "Yes."

"Are they sexually excited?"

"Erm, I'm not sure… Yes, I suppose so."

"And does that excite you Angela?"

"…yes!"

"Very good," Dave said. "This is how it's going to work Angela. I will meet you in a pub with your husband and my wife. If we all decide we want to progress things we will take it from there. Are you content with that?"

"Yes Master David."

"Good! Put your husband back on the phone and I'll make the arrangements with him."

The meeting was scheduled for Saturday evening; in two days time. Dave and Mel got to the Fox and Hound nice and early as they wanted to watch the other couple arrive. They set themselves up in the corner where Dave had a good view of the door and he got a pint of bitter and a fluorescent blue alcopop from the bar. Drew and Angela arrived bang on seven o'clock and Dave picked them out immediately. She was just stunning in a knee length summer dress and thin purple cardigan. Her lean and long body bulged in all the right places and her soft brown hair framed a face that attractive, sophisticated and a little haughty. Dave's cock jumped in his pants at the thought of manipulating her naked body. Drew was pretty nondescript. Average height, average looks and average build.

As the couple passed the table Dave stood so quickly to block their way that Angela nearly bumped into him and stopped with her bulging bosom only millimeters from his barrel chest. "Hello Angela," Dave said confidently. "It looks like you've found us," he added as he looked deep into her brown eyes from within her personal space. He gestured towards the seat. "Have a seat and introduce yourselves to Mel. I'll get you some drinks."

The couple sat and Dave went to the bar. "You look like a lager," Dave said to Drew as he put a pint in front of him. "And as for you, young lady, it had to be a slow screw against the wall."

The couple laughed nervously as he put the cocktail in front of her.

Dave let Angela make polite chat with Melanie for a while and he talked about sport and politics with Drew. He let that go for about thirty minutes and then took control of the conversation again. He reached across the conversation to get Angela's attention by touching her hand. "So Angela, tell me. Since you married, have you ever been intimate with anyone other than your husband?"

Angela and Drew exchanged nervous glances. "Er yes," she replied. "We gave swinging a go for a while but it didn't really work for us."

Dave let that one go for now but it was certainly a topic to explore later but he continued to probe. "Have you ever made love to another woman Angela?"

"No."

"More than one man at once?"

"No."

"Outside or somewhere else where there was a danger of being caught?"

"No."

"Have you taken a cock in your arse?"

"No."

"In your throat?"

"Not really."

"Do you swallow?"

"No."

"I like you, Angela," Dave said finally. "Would you like to be spanked this evening?"

"Yes please Master David," she said quietly without even looking at her husband.

The two couples travelled in Dave's BMW, leaving the teacher's Ford Focus parked in the pub car park. Melanie sat in the back with Drew, leaving Angela up front with her husband. Dave let his hand lightly brush against her knee several times as he changed gear but he didn't actually fondle her as it appeared he would. She kept her snooty expression and professional demeanour but the subtle clues told him she was a shot as hell. Her knees gradually slipped wider apart and her breathing deepened as they got closer to Dave's big house.

Dave entered first and switched off the alarm. He was aware of the closeness of Angela's body without even looking around. Since he had first met her only an hour or so before and invaded her personal space, she had hardly left it. He turned on the lights and led the way into a spacious kitchen, with a big oak table as the centerpiece. "Have a good look at the table," he said, turning to Angela. "You'll be getting to know it well in a few minutes. First of all though, you need to go and empty your bladder while you have the chance. Mel will show you the way."

As the girls made their way to the downstairs bathroom, Dave handed Drew a bottle of beer. "Put yourself on the other side of the table," he said. "Your job is to hold the lady by the wrists while I spank her. Think you can do that?"

"I'll manage," the smaller man replied.

"I've got to tell you Drew," continued Dave. "Your wife is delicious. I'm going to have to fuck her as well you know." The other man said nothing in reply so Dave continued. "Don't worry, she'll practically be begging for it by time I get inside her and whatever I do to her, you're free to get the same from Mel."

When the women returned, Melanie bent straight over the table without a word and offered her wrists up for Drew to hold. Dave flipped up her skirt to show a naked behind and beckoned a nervous Angela across to stand just to the right hand side of his woman's exposed rump. "You stand there and watch closely," he told her. "Mel will take everything you are going to get first so you know exactly what's going to happen. Okay?" Angela nodded dumbly in return.

Without any warning at all, Dave brought his hand down hard across his girlfriend's deceptively meaty left buttock. *Crack!* It was Angela who jumped at the loud sound; clearly imagining herself in that position, as she would be very shortly. Mel didn't so much as make a sound. Dave followed with six on each cheek; stopping when the white arse was glowing pink. He rested his hand on the hot skin and looked into Angela's eyes as he caressed his girlfriend.

"Do you think you can be as brave as Mel?" Dave asked as he continued to fondle. He saw Angela's eyes widen as his hand went lower and dipped into Melanie's honeypot. The inference was obvious. He had made it clear he would be duplicating everything he did to Melanie on her! He held his finger up in front of her so she could see the juices glisten in the light and smell his girlfriend's arousal. "Mel clearly enjoyed that little warm up," he laughed. "Your turn Angela. Slip your knickers off like a good girl."

Without any delay, for fear of annoying her new Master at this sensitive time, Angela reached into her skirt and tugged her panties down, bending over to pull them over her feet. Dave held out his hand for them and she duly handed them over.

As the tall woman bent over the table and let her husband grip her wrists, Dave placed her knickers over his face and inhaled deeply. "Mmmm! It looks like Mel isn't the only one who was creaming her pussy!" Angela's face began to redden and the turned to scarlet as she felt Dave's hands lift her skirt and expose her most private areas. His hand began to roam across her taut flesh; squeezing and stroking. "You are built for a good spanking my dear," he said in a complimentary tone. There's a bit of padding her but not too much. You're really going to feel this."

"Arrgh!" When the first slap connected, Angela couldn't help but let out a cry. It really hurt; a lot more than she had expected.

"Hold her tight," Dave commanded Angela's husband and began to let loose on her wriggling bottom. He was careful to give the novice exactly what Melanie had taken but she didn't take it nearly as well. Her breath was ragged and each exhale barely hid a sob. "Let's see how you enjoyed that," Dave said and the married woman knew exactly what was coming next as his middle finger brushed against the hairs around her pussy and slid inside her.

Dave took his time fingering the reluctant Angela, this time looking across at her husband as he slowly wriggled his finger around inside her. "She's very wet you know Drew," he smirked, drawing his finger out and sucking on it. "Tastes as sweet as honey too," he added. "Come and have a feel," he said to Melanie.

Angela was mortified as she felt the other woman's slim finger slip inside her. "Wow, she's very tight," she heard Melanie exclaim. "I hope you're going to fuck her. It'd be a waste not to!"

"We'll see," laughed Dave. "Now get in position and I'll whip that cheekiness out of you."

As Melanie changed places with Angela, Dave turned around and opened a cupboard in the corner. "I think we'll start with a strapping," he said as he selected a wide, supple leather belt.

The belt made a sound like a pistol shot as it connected with both of Melanie's buttocks at the same time. She didn't make a sound but the almost imperceptible jerk of her body gave an indication of her discomfort. Dave just gave her the six before he put the strap down. Without a word, he reached across and took Angela's hand; holding it against his girlfriend's pussy. "Is she gushing yet?"

Melanie looked over her shoulder. "You weren't told to put your fingers inside me," she sniggered and laughed again as Angela whipped her hand away as though she had been burned. This time, Dave took his time with Angela before he started to beat her. "I'm going to find your breaking point this evening my dear," he said as he cupped her soft buttocks. "Unless of course Melanie breaks first," he added, "but good luck with that one!"

Six hard licks of the strap were in fact almost enough to break the thirty three year old. Her legs began to rise in anticipation of the blows and she cried out each time it connected. "Ohhh!" Putting the belt away, Dave turned around to see his woman on her knees with her face buried in the teacher's box.

"No need to ask if that one made you moist," he chuckled. "Mel's clearly making a meal out of you!" He watched the woman's face closely. She was still in a little distress from the strapping and the idea of having another woman's mouth on her sex was overloading her senses. She writhed around on the table top and pulled against her husband's grip; which showed no sign of slackening. Dave let Mel eat her out for a few moments and then tapped her on the shoulder. "Come on little slut, it's your turn;" he encouraged her up on to the tabletop.

"I don't remember giving you permission to do that," he told his wife as he selected his next weapon. "Time for a punishment I think," he said, showing her a bamboo cane. Melanie went a little pale. She knew how much pain her master could inflict with one of these things and she was nervous for the first time. What tickled Dave was Angela's reaction. She sensed the younger woman's fear

11

and it had a knock on effect on her. She looked like a rabbit in the headlights!

Dave was really careful in applying the cane; he gave the already sore arse judiciously measured blows to avoid breaking the skin. All the same, ten blows was enough to bring her legs up in the 'spanking dance' and for a few errant tears to start rolling down her cheeks. "Well done my darling," he said soothingly as he patted her on the bottom and looked expectantly at Angela.

"Arrrgh!" Angela nearly brought the ceiling down with the first stroke. She pulled violently against her husband's grasp and very nearly got her wrists free.

"Calm down," Dave said soothingly, as his fingers wandered into her sopping wet twat again. He massaged her g spot for a while until she calmed down and then started again but a little less hard.

With the second blow, Angela's legs began to lift and the tears rolled down her face. By the time number ten came around, she was openly sobbing and begging for him to stop. Her lower body was moving so much, Dave had to pick his moment so he wasn't aiming for a moving target. He patted her on the bottom and dropped her skirt back down to give her back a little dignity. "You did well, sweetheart," he said "Now go with Mel and get cleaned up before we move things on a little.

When the girls had left the room, Dave got another couple of beers out the fridge and cracked them open. "She's a horny slut your wife," he said as he handed one over to Drew.

"I'll take that as a compliment, the younger man said in a non-committal voice.
"Take it however you like," sneered Dave, moving into the lounge with Drew following on. "We're going to give them twenty minutes," he continued as he collapsed into an armchair. "In that time my very talented woman will have your wife naked, blindfolded, tied to the bed and ripe for my cock. When we get up there' Mel's all yours. She'll fuck you rigid while I enjoy your innocent wife."

"Good luck with that," it was Drew's time to sneer. "There's no way Angela will let Melanie touch her. She's a black belt in karate you know!"

At that exact moment, Angela was whimpering into Melanie's mouth as the young woman rubbed her pussy with one hand. "No please," she moaned without conviction as she was allowed a moment to breath, "I don't think…".

Looking into the older woman's deep brown eyes, Melanie spoke softly to her. "Don't think," she said. "Just let things happen." Slipping the woman's cardigan off, she dropped it on to the floor and slowly began to unzip her dress.

Dave finished his second beer and got up from the chair. "Come on stud it's party time," he growled. Leading the other man up to the bedroom, he gave his girl a big smile as he entered. Melanie was sitting on the edge of the bed, gently rubbing lube into Angela's tight bum hole. The older woman was completely naked and blindfolded. She was on her front, with hands lashed securely to the rail at the top of the bed and her ankles cuffed together. Without a word, he pointed at a chair in the far corner of the room and Drew located himself there. Dave began to remove his own clothes while his girlfriend went to entertain their male guest.

Angela felt movement on the bed as Dave climbed up. She raised her head in an attempt to see through the blindfold but Dave had no intention of confirming who it was. Straddling her upper thighs, he dipped his hard cock into the pool of lubricant gel that Mel had left there and located her hole with the tip of his helmet.

With a barely imperceptible move of his hips, Dave shoved his eight inch cock deep inside the unsuspecting teacher. She lifted her head and let out a long wail. "Noooo!" He loved taking women in this position as the fact they were on their front with legs closed lulled them into a false sense of security. The fact was though, it afforded him the ideal position to be able to scrape his fat nobbly cock right along the girl's g spot. Grabbing her by the slim hips, he began to pump her hard.

Angela continued to complain. "Please no, my husband…" Without breaking his stride, Dave reached over and pulled off the woman's blindfold. She lifted her head and locked eyes on Drew. A naked Melanie was crouched in front of him and bobbing her head backwards and forwards to take his small cock into her throat. Dropping her head back to the bed in a sign of resignation, she surrendered herself to the intense feelings building deep inside her cunt as the big man behind her ploughed her deeply.

SUZI'S POLYAMOROUS MARRIAGE.

Suzi's marital bliss was beginning to tarnish again. She had been through a roller coaster of emotions with her beloved husband Damion. Succumbing to a submissive lifestyle to keep the marriage together had worked well for both of them and they had certainly strengthened their relationship by being intimate with others. There remained, however, one speed bump on the road to eternal bliss; Damion's mistress, Emma.

Despite the fact that all of her marriage problems had started with Emma, Suzi didn't hate her; far from it. Maybe she used to but she had got that out of her system some time ago. Besides, she fully recognized that Emma was the symptom and not the cause of the problems. Since those difficult days, they had met several times and had begun to build a proper friendship together, as well as the intimate one that Damion had instigated.

As she now had complete openness in her marriage with Damion, it was obvious to Suzi that he was beginning to spend an increasing amount of time away from her and with Emma. She was a pragmatist and could see why. She had spent a quarter of her life with her husband and they were very comfortable together. But comfort was often not what Damion wanted. Add to the mix the fact that Emma was extremely attractive and nearly ten years her junior and it wasn't difficult to see why Damion wanted to spend his time with her. She was as committed to him as ever and knew she had to make a bold move to keep him. Valentine's Day seemed like as good a time as ever to reveal her plan and she booked their favourite French restaurant.

Picking her moment after the dessert and their first bottle of wine, Suzi reached across the table and touched her husband's hand. "Damion," she ventured. "Be honest, do you still love me?"

Damion answered without hesitation. "Completely and without question, darling."

"And how do you feel about Emma?"

This time he paused before answering. "I like the way she makes me feel. I enjoy the fact that what I can experience with her complements what I get from you. She makes me happy."

"Do you love her?"

"In a way, yes, I suppose I do. It's different from the love I feel for you though… Sort of, more primal."

Suzi squeezed his hand and sighed. "I know all that you know and I've done my best to be all that you want but I'm worried... I'm worried that we're not going to grow old together." There was silence between the two of them for a few minutes as they sipped their wine. There was no point in trying to deny what they both felt. They knew each other much too well. It was Suzi who broke the silence again. "I may have a solution if you're prepared to consider it?"

The solution was simple. Damion should see Emma as often as he wanted to but it should involve Suzi wherever possible. That meant bringing her back home and for the three of them to get to know each other better together. Once Damion saw the sense in the idea, selling the concept to Emma was his problem but Suzi had no doubt he would get his way. He always did.

The following evening therefore had Suzi preparing a very special dinner party at home. The only guest was going to be Emma and Suzi was now very nervous about the idea. Although she had met the other woman twice before and on both occasions had fucked her like a bitch, this time was very different. She was welcoming her husband's mistress into her home as a friend and as an equal.

Emma was ten minutes late, which made Suzi inwardly smile. The younger woman was already emphasising the equality of their relationship. She looked absolutely stunning and had clearly spent a long time getting ready. As she stepped over the threshold, Suzi lightly held her shoulders and brushed her cheeks with her lips. "You look fantastic Emma," she said sincerely. "Please come in and make yourself at home."

Damion was no less complimentary but a little less refined. "You look like sex on legs sweetheart," he crooned, sweeping her into his arms. Suzi was intrigued to see that. She hadn't yet seen the way Damion and Emma interacted normally together but interestingly to her, she didn't feel even the slightest pang of jealousy when they embraced.

Dinner was delicious and the conversation soon flowed as freely as the wine. Damion felt he was on the periphery of the banter for possibly the first time ever as the girls bonded. The conversation swung from shoes to soap operas and he really didn't have a clue what they were talking about most of the time. He concentrated on keeping the wine glasses topped up and just chipped in when he could.

After dinner they moved through to the lounge and Damion brought the brandy bottle through. Emma stopped at a group of family pictures on the way. "These are your children aren't they? They are absolutely gorgeous."

Suzi just filled with happiness at that remark. However genuine it may or may not have been it hit the spot. There was no better way to her heart than through her children. "Thank you Emma, they are my angels. Sophie and Jonathan are both at boarding school."

Damion handed both women a glass of warming cognac. "Bottoms up ladies," he quipped.

"You first stud," answered Emma with a new confidence as she caught Suzi's eye.

"Yes," Suzi agreed. "Why not let the women take charge for a change darling? It'll make Emma feel a bit more at ease."

Damion laughed. "You are a pair of cheeky minxes all of a sudden aren't you! Fuck, why not . Okay, what do you want me to do"

"Strip bitch!" Suzi said unexpectedly, managing to keep the smile off her face. "Let's see your manly body."

Damion shrugged and pulled off his shirt and trousers. His lean body glistened in the firelight and his muscles flexed as he bent over to pull off his boxer shorts. Emma let out a low whistle, as though she was seeing her lover naked for the first time. "Look at the size of his cock Suzi," she murmured. "That'll make your eyes water."

Suzi bit her lip to stifle a laugh and then reached between her husband's legs, squeezing his cock. "You are a big boy aren't you," she said as she pulled and manipulated him.

"Big enough," Damion chuckled as he let his wife take the lead.

"Where do you keep the cuffs Suz?" Emma asked, as she added her small hand to her new best friend's; cupping Damion's hairy scrotum.

"What a great idea," Suzi laughed, leaving the two of them together while she went up to the bedroom to collect a few things.

When she returned, Emma had moved things on a bit. She was naked from the waist down and spread across the sofa; holding Damion by the head and encouraging him to eat her out. "Well this party certainly started without me," she said as she dropped a heavy bag on to the floor. Reaching inside, she found a pair of police handcuffs, pulled Damion's strong arms behind his back and cuffed them in place.

The boot was now very firmly on the other foot, if only for a while. All the same, the girls were going to make the most of it. Suzi reached around and began to slowly wank her husband's cock as Emma shoved his face into her gushing pussy. "What do you think Emma?" the older woman asked over her husband's shoulder. "Shall I peg him?"

"I don't know about that," Emma laughed, "but I'm definitely having the first ride of that magnificent prick. Help me get him on his back."

The women manoeuvred the big man over so he was lying on his back across the couch and left him alone while they disrobed. Suzi watched her friend as she slipped off her bra and had to compliment her. "You're a very beautiful woman you know, Emma. You're quite irresistible."

"Well don't resist me then," Emma laughed, taking the older woman's hands and placing them on her small but perfectly formed breasts.

"Mmmm," Suzi sighed. "I love the feel of your tits in my hands." Leaning forward, she nibbled on Emma's soft lips before taking her mouth with her own as the younger women unclipped her own bra and slipped it off her shoulders.

"I could make love to you all night darling," Emma murmured into Suzi's mouth.

"Me too," replied Suzi and we'll definitely do that. But first, we have a very full sack to empty," she said, gesturing to the side, where she was still slowly rubbing her husband's swollen cock. "Why don't you climb on?" She held the cock upwards while Emma climbed aboard it and gave her clitoris a few loving rubs as she settled herself down.

As Emma began to move slowly up and down with the big cock inside her, Suzi straddled her husband's face and gently cupped her lover's breasts. Gasping as she felt Damion's tongue inside her, she offered her mouth to Emma again and the three of them came together in a triangle of passion.

Suzi focussed on the amazing feelings inside her pussy as Damion's mouth turned her inside out. Moaning inside Emma's mouth, she was aware of the other woman's passion as her hips began to buck faster and she started getting really vocal. She leant further over and embraced Emma properly, supporting her head on her shoulder as she assisted her movement up and down.

When Emma's orgasm came, it was as though a dam had burst. "Oh my God yes! Yes! Yeees!" She threw her head back and screamed as Damion's cock pulsed and spat a big load of spunk deep inside her.

"Ooooooh!" Suzi mashed her soggy cunt all over her husband's face as her body convulsed and she came too. She could feel the juices flowing out of her and into Damion's open mouth as her orgasm seemed to go on forever. She collapsed on to Damion's face, still holding tightly to her girlfriend as she felt the tension drift out of her muscles; only moving when her husband's urgent movements jerked her back to reality as she realised she was suffocating him. Jumping off, she held out her hand to help Emma dismount and then rolled Damion on to his side to release the cuffs. Kissing him on the lips, she thanked him. "Why don't you turn the rugby on sweetheart while Emma and I go upstairs and get better acquainted?" she offered, taking the other woman by the hand and leading her upstairs.

Over the course of the following few weeks, Suzi and Emma began spending more and more time together until they reached the point where they were seeing each other every day. At that point there was an obvious next step. Suzi popped the question when the three of them were having a lazy Sunday morning in bed. "Damion and I have been thinking," she murmured as she caressed the soft hair of the head on her chest. "It seems pointless you driving half an hour back to your flat every night and we've got plenty of space here…

"I'd love to," Emma said quickly. "If you're sure that is? There's the children to think of as well…"

"The kids will love you," Suzi answered, kissing her on the forehead. "Why wouldn't they? We do!"

"Okay. I'll bring my stuff over next weekend,"

"Bring your stuff whenever you like," Damion chipped in, squeezing her naked bottom from behind. "We're keeping you from now on."

"I'm going to enjoy being your second wife," she chirped, turning over and shuffling down the bed to take Damion's meat into her mouth. Letting the cock drop out for a moment, she reached up to squeeze Suzi's hand. "And yours too of course," she added.

The three of them spent six months together in conjugal bliss. Emma chipped in with the housework when she could, outside her work hours and insisted on paying a share of the utility bills, although it was hardly necessary. And then she dropped the bombshell. "Suz," she said over breakfast. "I've just had a positive test."

Suzi knew immediately what she was talking about. She reached across the table and took both of her hands in her own. "Emma. That's wonderful darling."

"I suppose so," said Emma hesitantly. "It's just that I've always wanted a baby but imagined I would be married first."

"Oh Emma," Suzi gushed, coming around the table and hugging her from behind. "I know what you mean but you don't need to worry. We both love you so much and we'll love your baby too you know."

"I suppose so," Emma sighed. "Thank you," she added and turned to kiss her friend on the lips.

As the pregnancy progressed, Emma's hormones went through the roof and the married couple took full advantage of that fact. She was fucked by Damion before they went to work in the morning and when he got back at night. She often managed her daily routine to nip back and spend an hour of passion at lunchtime or in the afternoon and the evening was always topped off with a threesome. This daily routine continued for several months; just modified when the children were home for their holidays and as predicted, they got on with their new aunty like a house on fire.

One Saturday morning, Suzi heard a little squeal from the bathroom and rushed in, thinking her girlfriend was in trouble. Far from it though. The squeal was one of excitement as she had discovered her milk had come in. "Oh, baby," Suzi laughed, as she kissed her. "Damion's going to love this. You'll be his special dessert tonight."

Damion was late home that night and more than a little stressed from work problems. Suzi saw him coming and met him with a scotch and a kiss. "I've got your favourite for dinner tonight," she told him.

"Steak and chips?" he asked hopefully.

"Steak and chips…and milk pudding," Suzi giggled.

"Mistress milk?"

"You betcha!"

The steak went down very easily. The girls had already eaten and so just waited on their Master hand and foot. They both looked delectable in short skirts and peasant blouses, such that Damion found it hard to concentrate on his food with his cock tenting his trousers. Finally he finished the last morsel and Suzi whipped his plate away, leaving him with just his wine glass.

Suzi turned Emma to face him and gently caressed her swollen belly. "Ready for dessert? She asked cheekily.

"Always!"

"Well just you sit there for now and enjoy the show," Suzi said in a low, sultry voice as she moved her hands upwards to squeeze Emma's engorged breasts. She slowly and firmly massaged the firm globes as she nuzzled her girly's neck. Emma started to squirm under the older woman's touch, her senses finely honed; fuelled by her over-active hormones. As Damion watched intently, she slowly unlaced the young woman's blouse and unclipped the front fastening bra, holding her ripe tits out towards him. "Look very carefully my darling," she murmured as she squeezed the fat nipples towards him, releasing a drop of milk.

"Mmmm!" Damion exclaimed. "Fresh milk straight from the teat!" Rising from his seat, he took the young woman into his arms and dropped his head to her breast, sucking a nipple straight into his mouth.

"Oooh yes!" Emma practically squealed at the feeling of warm milk leaving her tit. Grabbing her Master's head in both arms, she held him tightly as he sucked her hard. Suzi busied herself with removing Emma's clothes as Damion enjoyed her milk, dropped her skirt and peeling down her panties. As Damion switched to the other breast, Suzi reached around Emma's hip and began to lightly circle her clitoris.

"Oh my God!" Emma yelled. "for Christ sake fuck me before I explode!"

Damion guided the girl over to the table and lifted her up on to it. Hooking his arms under her knees and pulling her close, she bent forward to continue to suckle for her milk as Suzi reached between them to slot her husband's rigid cock into Emma's hungry pussy. With an almost imperceptible movement of his hips, Damion pushed himself inside her velvety love tunnel.
Damion screwed his young lover slowly and tenderly, suckling on one breast while Suzi fed on the other. He gazed down on her exposed body as he moved inside her; his tender but firm movements pushing her backwards and forwards along the wooden table top. Her body had changed hugely in the past few weeks. Her distended belly rose up like a hilly mound, her full bosoms proud and firm; the nipples and areolae some three times their original size. She was larger but incredibly beautiful; ripe and womanly. He held her firmly by the hips and drilled his big cock into her tight cunny.

When Emma came, it was less violent but more intense than usual. He continued to move inside her as her orgasm concluded and then withdrew to let his kneeling wife take the full load in her mouth. Sweeping his pregnant lover into his arms he carried her to bed; accompanied by his wife.

Suzi kissed their sleeping mistress on the lips and covered her with the duvet before turning to her husband. "I think we've found the perfect love triangle," she sighed as she snuggled into his arms. It took a while to get there but Suzi was now content she had the ideal marriage.

THE MILKING MACHINE.

Carrie couldn't believe her luck. She had nailed the best gap year job imaginable. The pay was outstanding, the work and hours were easy and it was in the countryside; on a dairy farm to be precise. For this country girl who had been stuck in the middle of Edinburgh at university for three years, that alone was a good enough reason to take it.

The farmer was the cousin of her dad's best friend, so it was probably a bit of a *shoo in* as a favour really. The interview was dead easy and lasted about twenty minutes. Once Joel, the farm manager learned that her degree was in farm management, he was more than happy to take her on for the year. She almost regretted spending nearly three hundred pounds on the *oh so sexy but still professional* skirt, blouse and high heels combination that had held his attention from the moment she walked in.

She started the very next day, arriving in her Ford Fiesta at nine o'clock, dressed in a far more suitable combination of jeans and t shirt. Even dressed casually, the twenty one year old blonde looked as hot as hell and she knew it. The farm was packed with young, muscular studs and she was apparently the only woman around. If she couldn't snare a horny farmhand, she wanted to know why not. Her slim five foot six body, long legs and perky tits had certainly got their fair share of attention.

Joel showed her round himself before she started. He ran through the boring health and safety stuff about accidents and fire assembly points and then explained how the farm worked, showing her the milking sheds and pastures. Stopping at the far side of the yard, he pointed out a smaller shed with a locked door. "This is the quarantine shed," he said with a serious voice. "Under no circumstances are you to go in there."

Carrie nodded her agreement and continued to follow him round, back into the big office building. They finished up in his office, where he had set her aside a desk. He then took a few minutes to run through the computerized stock control program. It would be her primary responsibility to monitor stock and ensure the farm operated within required parameters, he explained. Carrie chucked her rucksack in the corner of her cubicle, grabbed a coffee and started to get her head around the software.

The morning flew by and Carrie wasn't short of visitors to her side of the office. She met at least a dozen young men before lunch. They were all gorgeous and to a man they all flirted with her shamelessly; invariably being thrown out by Joel when they had outstayed their welcome and needed to go back to work. In between these visits and the chats with her equally handsome boss, Carrie got to grips with the accounting system. Once she had an understanding of the spreadsheets, something began to puzzle her. The unit price of one of the products, something called Gold Standard was outrageously expensive. In fact it was five time the price of all of the other product lines. There was clearly a mistake.

Joel was quite dismissive with her when she pointed it out. "Don't worry, there's no mistake. That's a very special type of milk."

Carrie thought nothing more of it and got on with her work. The day flew by. Joel took her down to the staff canteen for lunch and she had another half hour of being the centre of attention before she felt obliged to make her excuses and return to work. Halfway through the afternoon, she was visited by apparently the only other woman on the complex, the owner's wife, a lady in her late thirties called Margherita. Carrie found her a little strange. Stunningly attractive and svelte, she seemed to just come to look at her, rather than build a relationship. Carrie almost felt like a zoo animal being examined behind bars.

The next day, Carrie dressed down even more. She was determined to end her romantic drought and one of these hunks of man flesh had her name on; she just didn't know which one yet. Pulling on a leather mini skirt and crop top, she had a quick look in the mirror and then decided to go one step further. Pulling off her top, she removed her bra before covering back up again. Her little pebbles showed cleared through the thin cotton but her tits were quite firm enough to support themselves. Overall the look was sexy, without being slutty. She was quite happy that she'd make the right impression and hurried out of her flat.

Joel went for a wander around the farm in the middle of the morning and he had hardly left the building when his phone rang. Carrie answered it. "Hello, Joel's phone can I help you?"

"And who is this?" a smooth foreign voice asked.

"Erm, it's Carrie," she replied hesitantly. "I've just started here."

"That's very nice my dear," the unknown voice continued. "I very much look forward to meeting you. Now, I must talk with Joel straight away. Could you put him on please."

"Oh, I'm sorry," she replied. "He's just popped out. "Can I take a message?"

"Could you please find him without delay and ask that he calls Ahmed?"

Carrie put the phone down and rushed out. The yard was big but not that big and she was sure she'd find him pretty fast.

Alas, twenty minutes later, she'd looked just about everywhere without success. He wasn't in the milking sheds or the production facility. She looked all around the yard and eventually found herself outside the big barn she had been forbidden to enter. There were several pedestrian doors and the closest one was ajar. She paused and thought about things before continuing. Joel had said not to enter because it was a quarantine area. She was very familiar with quarantine procedures from her studies and was sure she could enter without placing the animals at risk and Ahmed said it was essential she found Joel as quickly as possible. She carefully checked her shoes for dirt and debris and stepped over the threshold.

It was very gloomy inside and Carrie needed a few seconds for her eyes to adjust. There was a steady hum of machinery and sighs and moans that sounded almost … human. There was something very odd about this place and Carrie was intrigued. The big shed was draped with plastic curtains and she could just make out indistinct shapes moving inside. She had to know more. Taking a deep breath, she stepped up to the closest curtain and pulled it aside.

Carrie was really not prepared for what she saw. There was a young woman, perhaps two or three years older than she was, lying naked on a sort of hospital bed. Her legs were in stirrups; splaying her obscenely and her breasts were covered by big transparent rubbery things that she could only describe as suckers. As she looked harder, she realised they were moving and pumping what could only be milk from the poor girl's breasts. Was she pregnant? She looked down at the woman's stomach, which was stretched tautly over washboard abs, then she quickly averted her gaze as she found her eyes drawn to the moist open petals of her pussy. She then caught the woman's eyes and was shocked to see a blissful, even bovine expression in her face. She was actually enjoying this!

Suddenly Carrie was aware of a presence behind her and her slim shoulders were grasped in a strong grip. "I thought I told you to keep out of here you silly girl," Joel's voice boomed.

Carrie's heart dropped into her shoes. She had uncovered something very wrong and suddenly she was in the middle of it. She began to panic and struggled against Joel's grip. Two more men appeared at her side and held her arms. They were both familiar to her as farm workers. Joel released her shoulders and stroked her cheek. "Calm down kitten," he said softly. "We're not going to hurt you so take a few deep breaths."

The terrified young woman was part dragged, part carried back to the office complex. Rather than going upstairs to Joel's office though, they entered a door on the ground floor and Carrie found herself in a big, whitewashed room. The room was empty apart from some sort of examination table right in the middle, with hose and wires leading from it into a big cylinder that sat against the wall. Her trepidation grew as she was dragged across to it, pushed on to her back and her arms firmly strapped down.

The other men stepped back, leaving Carrie looking directly at Joel and to her horror, she saw he had a sharp knife in his hand. "Don't panic," he chuckled, sensing her fear. "I said I wouldn't hurt you and I meant it." Stepping forward, he pulled her crop top away from her body and sliced through it with the razor sharp blade, pushing the remnants to either side to fully expose her perky tits. "Hmmm, did you forget your bra this morning?" he asked with a smile. "Very nice though," he murmured appreciatively, brushing his thumbs across her nipples to make them stand up to attention.

Joel busied himself at a console just out of sight, starting up the machine and shuffling some items around. Moments later, he appeared back in Carrie's eye line, holding a fearsome looking hypodermic needle. "This going to make you feel really good," he chuckled as he prepared the injection. "There's a bit of a mixture in here," he continued as the needle slid into the relaxed muscle on the underside of her arm. "We've experimented for months to find the perfect formula. As well as a powerful milk production stimulator, there's an aphrodisiac and weak sedative."

Carrie's head began to swim and she felt really relaxed all of a sudden. It was almost an out of body experience. She was vaguely aware of Joel removing her panties and fastening her legs up high in stirrups. She realised she must be spread open as widely as the girl in the shed. Joel was messing around with the apparatus between her legs and then suddenly she felt something firm, warm and blunt lodge between her labia. Next, Joel switched on the machine and held cups over her breasts until they sucked into place. Then she felt the thing pushing against her pussy start to buzz and move slowly inside her.

"Let me explain what's happening," said Joel. "Now the machine's on, it's completely automatic. It is equipped with sensors which give the computer a wide variety of information about your body and it will adjust its stimulation until your body starts to produce milk… And it will," he added, seeing the disbelief in Carrie's eyes.

Joel left the room and Carrie was on her own with the infernal machine. The dildo, or whatever it was burrowing its way into her vulva; gently stretching her young pussy walls. She already felt fuller than ever before and it was only half way in. Her whole body was tingling and she felt just fantastic. Oddly, she realised she was no longer scared and her whole focus was on the tingling feeling starting in between her legs.

All of a sudden, Carrie was aware of her breasts. The suction cups were constantly moving in a sort of milking action and she felt her nipples being alternately tugged up into the cups. It was a little sore but in a nice way. All the same, she felt like shouted at the dumb machine, there's no milk, so stop trying to milk me.

Suddenly her attention was switched back to her cunt. The dildo was jammed right inside her and seemed to be growing. She really did feel stuffed in a way she had only imagined before. The thick phallus withdrew slowly and then, without warning, slammed back into her. Her back arched as much as the equipment allowed and she let out a howl of pain and passion, "Oooooh!"

Joel was watching Carrie's progress through a monitor. She was a fever pitch he saw and likely to come at any time. He had broken in a wide variety of women on the machine now and it didn't matter whether they were old, young, loose, frigid, haughty or shy, they all reacted in exactly the same way. Once their pussy was sufficiently primed, their brains were effectively reprogrammed. Several hundred years of female evolution wiped out by a small injection and a big rubber cock he laughed to himself.

As Joel checked Carrie's readings, the door opened and a young woman stepped through. "Hello Georgina," he greeted her warmly. "How was your milking this morning?"

The buxom redhead was scantily dressed and had a fire in her eyes. "It was mind blowing as always and I'm horny as hell as usual," she purred. "I've come to see if that beautiful penis of yours is available."

"I'm a little busy with the new girl," Joel answered, "so come over here and blow me for now."

Georgina sashayed across and sank to her knees. A beautiful young woman with piercing blue eyes and skin that glowed, she had been a brilliant linguist before she entered Joel's milking programme. Now her past didn't matter. She was Joel's favourite milker and shagger. All that mattered to her was the feelings she got from milking and sex. She unzipped her Master's fly and took his substantial cock in her little white hand, wanking it slowly a few times before wrapping her hot lips around it. "Mmmmm!" she moaned around it.

Joel tried to keep his concentration on the computer screen in front of him. He could see Carrie was very close and didn't want to miss the moment. The shiny red hair flying around his groin area, however, caught his attention, as did the soft and insistent suction on his cock. Eventually, it was too much. He held Georgina's head gently but firmly in his hands and began to thrust into her accommodating throat.

Just as Joel felt himself about to spill over, an alarm sounded on the console. That was it, Carrie's milk was about to come. Pushing the redhead away so he clipped out of her mouth, he pushed his cock away with difficulty and zipped up. "Sorry sweetheart, there's an even needier young lady next door," he said as he helped her to her feet.

"Oooh! Oooh! Oooh!" Carrie was out of control. The machine was fucking her savagely with a rubber cock far bigger than any her pussy had taken before and her tits were being relentlessly mauled. Her hips came off the bench so that her lower body was suspended on by the stirrups and her pussy convulsed around the hard rubber as she came harder than she could ever remember before. Her orgasm continued with no signs of abatement as the machine continued its nefarious work. The intensity grew and her whole body began to tingle when suddenly something happened. Her tits began to really throb; they became quite painful. That feeling grew and grew until it was almost unbearable and then a dam seemed to burst. Fireworks exploded behind her eyes and the orgasm hit her breasts. "Oh My Fucking God! Yes!"

As Carrie started to come down, she realised that the dildo had withdrawn from her and the suction cups were steadily sucking milk from her bosoms. Yes milk! She could clearly see the white fluid running up the tubes and she actually felt it leave her sensitive nipples.

She felt a rough hand stroke her soft inner thigh and looked up to see Joel standing between her legs with a stunning redhead just behind him. "Welcome to the herd, Carrie," he said. "How are you feeling?"

"Incredibly horny," she answered honestly.

"Well, let me help you out with that Joel laughed. "It's the least I can do." Releasing her ankles from the stirrups, he held them up instead and Carrie felt his cockhead searching for her young slit. Her milk flow had just about finished and as Joel entered her, she saw the redhead turn off the machine and remove the suction cups from her throbbing boobs.

Georgina replaced the cups with her soft lips and fingers. "What bra size were you before?" she asked between mouthfuls of sweet milk.

"34B," Carrie answered without even thinking.

Georgie chuckled. "You'll find you're more like a 34C now!"

As Carrie tried to get her head around that, Joel's meaty cock broke into her twat. Despite her earlier fucking by the machine, she still felt very tight around him. She could feel every ridge and bump on his knobby penis as it tunnelled its way inside her warm, velvety vulva. He reached down and grabbed her slim hips with his big string hands and began to pound her hard.

Carrie lasted less than a minute before her body started to convulse again. She bucked and writhed between her two tormentors before her pussy clamped down hard on Joel's meat, pushing him into his own climax.

"Fuck yes!" the big man exclaimed as he blew his wad inside the young woman's delicious body. As he withdrew, Georgina detached herself from feeding at Carrie's breasts and dropped to her knees to thoroughly clean Joel's cock, before noisily slurping up the combined juices that were leaking from the younger woman's cunt.

"I hope you enjoyed that," Joel said as he zipped up, "'cos there's plenty more to come."

Carrie refocused on the room and saw a sea of male faces. It seemed that the entire workforce had turned out to watch the boss hump her.

"The tradition around here is that everyone gets to fuck a new dairy girl on her first day!"

Carrie thought about that for a moment and decided she couldn't think of a better way to spend the afternoon; as the next cock found her messy opening.

THE STUDENT'S MOTHER.

Middle-aged millionaire Jeremy had seen his young student, Michelle regularly since dressing her as a cow and taking her to an orgy. Although his other girlfriends were classically more beautiful than the voluptuous nineteen year old, she was just a great fuck. She remained tight, however many cocks went through her and she was just so submissive and malleable; and always so grateful that she invariably left him wanting more.

That evening he had her tied to her coffee table. Her thighs were splayed wide and tied to the legs. Her big tits were squished against the glass table top and her wrists were secure behind her back. He was entertaining himself by smacking her arse with a wooden spatula he had found in the kitchen. It made a delightful *thwack* as it hit her meaty arse and was doing a good job of reddening it up. All the same, he didn't think it stung that much; certainly nothing like the cane he had introduced her to the previous week.

Once her arse was glowing pink all over, Jeremy dropped to his knees behind her and lined up his hard cock with her pink little slit. Pushing inside her snug little tunnel felt as great as ever and elicited the usual vocal effect. Holding her firmly by her soft hips, he smashed her pelvis against the edge of the table as he fucked the cute student hard and fast.

Once he had satisfied himself inside her, Jeremy moved around the table and offered his sticky cock for the submissive girl to clean. "Good girl," he encouraged, ruffling her soft hair, as Michelle enthusiastically licked and sucked their combined juices off his knob. He untied her and rubbed the rope marks to help the circulation. "Come on then," he smacked her arse in a more friendly manner than earlier. "Get me a beer!"

Half an hour later, they were snuggled up on the sofa watching a film like romantic lovers. Michelle clearly had something on her mind and Jeremy gave her permission to speak freely.

"Do you mind not coming around tomorrow?" she asked plaintively.

"Why?"

"My mother is visiting and it might be a bit difficult to explain our, erm relationship."

Jeremy got up and snatched a framed photograph off the mantelpiece and had a good look at the older woman stood next to Michelle. "Is this her?"

"Yes, Sir."

"Right. This is what we're going to do..."

The following afternoon, Jeremy was in his Lamborghini. He pulled up outside the flat and smiled to himself as he saw the curtain twitch. Michelle had clearly primed the pump as he'd directed. Sure enough, it was her mother who answered the door. He stepped back and appraised the older woman. He guessed she was around thirty eight, some four years younger than he was. She was about five feet six and very slim; and very attractive. Although she had a completely different body shape to her daughter, it was very clear where the big tits had come from but they looked even better on this delicate frame. "Hello," he said with mock surprise. "Who are you?"

"I'm Michelle's mother," she answered. "And you must be the landlord."

"I'm Jeremy," he said, holding out his hand formally.

"Monica," she replied, accepting the handshake.

Jeremy let himself in and greeted Michelle with an unemotional hello. He sat down on the sofa and looked at the younger woman expectantly.

"I'll put the kettle on," Michelle said and rushed into the kitchen.

"You've obviously done very well for yourself Jeremy," Monica said, trying unsuccessfully to keep a condescending tone from her voice.

"I do alright," he chuckled. "What about you Monica?" he leaned over and fixed her with the seductive stare that he knew always made women shift in their seat. "Where are you from and what do you do?"

"I live in Trowbridge," she replied. "I have a flower arranging business and I'm a town councillor." That was nothing that Jeremy didn't already know but be pretended to be impressed. Monica then quickly shifted the conversation. "I believe my daughter is in arrears with her rent?"

At that very moment, Michelle crashed through the door with three mugs of tea so Jeremy changed the conversation again. "You've been busy around the flat Michelle," he said. "The place looks fantastic."

"Thank you, Jeremy," Michelle gushed as she handed out the tea.

The three of them made small talk as they sipped their tea. Having covered the weather, Michelle's studies and the mechanics of flower arranging, they came back to the elephant in the room. "Can you give me a few minutes alone with your mother, Michelle," Jeremy asked, in their pre-planned ploy. Before her mother could protest, Michelle got up and quickly left the room.

Jeremy focused all of his attention on her mother, sitting just a little closer to her on the couch. "I haven't been entirely honest with you Monica," he began.

"Oh," came the nervous reply. "How exactly?"

"Michelle doesn't owe me for rent arrears exactly and I'm not exactly her landlord. At least not in the conventional manner." He paused to watch her reaction. "She's my mistress."

"Whaaat!"

"That's right, Mrs Tyler. I fuck your daughter."

Monica's face flushed with anger and she tried to stand; unsuccessfully. Her legs turned to jelly and she fell back on to the sofa and into Jeremy's arms. "What the hell have you done to me? And get your hands off me!"

"I haven't done anything to you Monica but your daughter slipped a little something into you tea to make you more… malleable. Now look at the screen, I've got something to show you." He grabbed the TV remote and flicked on a DVD that was ready on pause. Monica's jaw nearly hit the ground as the film started to play and she saw her beloved daughter dressed as a cow, being repeatedly fucked by men and women alike.

Monica watched in silence at her little girl being violated over and over again. Finally, as the film finished she turned to her tormentor. "What do you want?" she asked quietly.

Jeremy placed his hand on her knee and ran it lightly up her inner thigh, underneath her woollen skirt. "Why you, of course Monica," he replied simply.

The penny dropped and Monica brushed his hand away. "You have got to be joking," she retorted. "I'm a respectable married woman."

Jeremy laughed. "No, you're a respectable separated woman," he said. "And I'm willing to bet you haven't had any cock for a good while." He moved his hand to her shoulder and caressed her gently through her silky blouse. "Now then, are you feeling a little strange? Yes, well let me explain my darling. First of all, the drug that your darling daughter has administered to you will stop your legs working for about half an hour but more importantly it is a very strong aphrodisiac and right now should be making your tits throb and your pussy tingle. Does that sound about right?"

Monica didn't answer but shifted in her seat, so Jeremy continued. "More importantly, I know your council website and your local community Facebook page so I wonder what impact posting this video would have."

"Are blackmailing me?" Monica asked quietly.

"If you like," Jeremy laughed. "The thing is Monica," he said as his hand moved to one of her big, firm breasts. "Thing is, I have a large amount of money and an even bigger sex drive. I like to use the former to enhance the latter, if you know what I mean. I'm going to fuck you my dear and it's up to you whether you enjoy it or not." He began to unbutton her blouse.

Monica was speechless. She felt completely powerless to react. Her body was tingling in the grasp of this powerful man and she had a fire starting between her legs. She lay back and let him manipulate her, trying hard to forget her daughter in the next room.

Jeremy quickly had her blouse unbuttoned and reached behind her back to unhook her bra, capturing a nipple in his mouth as the big bosom fell free. Reaching between her legs and up her skirt, he thrust two fingers into her hairy cunt, enjoying the fact that it was sopping wet. Without further delay, he grabbed the woman by the hips and dragged her towards him on the couch, letting her legs spread out around him. Grabbing her sensible knickers in one hand, he ripped them from her body in one violent motion; the little scream telling him he had a handful of pubes too. In one smooth movement he freed up his cock and impaled it up to the hilt in the warm and moist pussy.

"Arrgh!" Monica was filled with a gamut of emotions, along with this wonderful penis. She felt ashamed, scared, embarrassed and very, very horny. It had been a long time since she'd had a man inside her and her entire focus was now on the incredible feelings in her pussy. She realised her hips had begun moving by themselves; rotating up to meet the savage thrusts of this horrible man who was molesting her. His hands had moved to her breasts and his was squeezing them really hard but by Christ it was good.

Jeremy humped the horny woman as hard and fast as he could. He could feel her passion being transmitted through her twat and into his cock. He felt incredibly big and hard and knew he couldn't last for long. Sure enough, in no time at all he felt his balls tightening and the tell tale twitch in his cock. He leaned forward to nibble the reluctant milf's lower lip and then whispered to her, "I'm going to fill your womb with boiling hot spunk Mrs Tyler. What do you think of that?"

Monica's whole body stiffened. "Christ no! I'm not on the pill, you can't, pull out!"

It was too late. Jeremy had passed the point of no return and couldn't pull out even if he wanted to. He gripped her tits so hard she screamed, thrust in so far his bell end touched her cervix and came with a roar. His balls emptied far inside her and the flow seemed to last forever. Monica found herself consumed with emotion and her body took control. Her vagina convulsed and clamped around the fat cock she screamed out her orgasm. "Oooooh! Oh my God, yes!"

Monica took a while to recover. She felt Jeremy withdraw from her and she lay back to get her breath back and give her head chance to stop spinning. When she opened her eyes, the first thing she saw was her daughter with a camcorder glued to her face. "What the hell are you doing?" she exclaimed.

"She's doing what I want her to, as always," intervened Jeremy. "That's something you're going to learn. Now how are your legs?" he took her hand and pulled her to her feet.

She was still shaky but Monica found she could stand. She let Jeremy lead her off to her daughter's bedroom; Michelle following close behind, still filming.

Jeremy left his milf stood in the middle of the bedroom floor and sat on the bed. "We have some wonderful footage of you asking for more cock," he said. "We'll edit that in with the other stuff later, should we need it if you start cooperating. Are you going to stop cooperating Monica?"

"No!"

"Good, strip for the camera!" Monica slipped her blouse and bra off her shoulders and then eased her skirt down her thighs; standing in front of her new lover and her own daughter dressed only in heels. "You are a very beautiful woman Monica," Jeremy said appreciatively, "now come here and kneel down."

Monica crept across the carpet and dropped slowly to her knees, finding herself inches away from Jeremy's flaccid but still intimidating cock. He said nothing more but it was very clear what he wanted. Her delicate hand was shaking as she grasped the sticky prick and held it up to her mouth. She took a couple of breaths and then her lips parted and she took it inside.

"Oh yes," Jeremy encouraged, as he gripped her head with both hands. "That feels awesome you filthy little slut." Monica froze for a moment at his words. Filthy little slut? No one had ever spoken to her like that before but then she was naked on her knees, sucking her own juices from a stranger's penis, in front of her own daughter and on camera. That was probably just what she was. She pushed the thought to one side and concentrated on the job at hand. She never used to perform oral sex on her ex-husband and didn't think she was particularly good at it but this horrible man was very demanding. He was holding her head hard and pulling it onto himself so hard she could actually feel the end touching the back of her throat.

Jeremy was really enjoying this blow job. It was by no means the most professional one he'd ever had but it was clear he was breaking new ground with this naïve housewife. He pushed into her warm throat and she gagged, so he withdrew a little before pushing in again to get a similar result. Starting a steady pumping motion had her gagging and spluttering and drool began to stream down her chin. He was now hard as iron once more.

He could quite easily have blown his load down Monica's throat but he had another idea in mind. "I'm going to have your arse next sweetheart," he announced as the helpless woman had his cock lodges in her throat. "Will I be your first?"

"Nggug! Nggug!" she exclaimed in an unintelligible reply that was clearly negative. When Jeremy lifted her bodily off the floor, she found the power of speech again. "Please don't do that, it's disgusting... I never have... it will hurt so much."

"Don't worry little one, I'm very good at it, just ask your daughter" he laughed as he laid her on her front on Michelle's bed. Monica looked up to see that Michelle was still filming and let her head drop on to her hands. She just lay there, stunned as Jeremy opened Michelle's bedside drawer and dug out the slippery lube he had left there a few nights ago. She jumped a little as the cold gel touched her hot anus but said nothing.

Moments later, Jeremy's heavy bulk straddled the back of Monica's thighs and she felt an insistent nudging at her sensitive rosebud. He was going to actually do it. She had never even contemplated anything quite so disgusting but now she was at the threshold, she was actually quite keen on the idea. The pressure on her ring piece steadily increased until, finally, her sphincter gave in and the meaty cock broke through.

There was a little pain; a sort of sharp sensation that took her latent memory straight back twenty odd years to when she lost her virginity in the back of a Ford Escort. And then she just felt very full. Jeremy's strong hands gripped her shoulders for leverage and pulled her backwards as he thrusted. She felt every millimetre of penetration as the big meat cylinder opened up her back passage and when it bottomed out, she thought her eyes were going to pop out of her head. It was odd, disgusting but fucking glorious!

Jeremy was having a great time. He looked up and winked at Michelle; who was still filming the action as he humped her mum's deliciously tight bum hole. He loved that the young student was so completely in his power as to give up her mother's virtue so easily. He also loved nothing more than taking the last virginity of a mature, worldly woman like Monica. A woman who thought she had explored the boundaries of her sexual desire already and just had no idea that she hadn't even started the journey yet.

The slap, slap, slap of Jeremy's hard thighs hitting the woman's soft buttocks filled the room; punctuated by guttural little moans, each time he bottomed out. Her anus was clenched hard around his cock and her bottom rose up to meet him in a very obvious statement of intent. He held her firmly and buggered so hard the sweat poured off his forehead and on to her flawless back.

"Uh! Uh! Uh!" Monica's moans got louder and more passionate. Her whole body was on fire and her tortured arsehole was the centre of an impending explosion. Every molecule in her body seemed fully charged and geared towards one end. Her orgasm was coming. It was going to hit hard and there was nothing that could stop it.

Jeremy felt it too. Looking up at Michelle, he gasped out a command. "Make sure you film her face!" he hardly got the words out when Monica's arsehole clenched hard around him and she convulsed in the most powerful orgasm of her life. Her body began to shudder and she screamed out her passion. "Oh God! Oh God! Oh God! Yes! Fucking Yeees!"

The vice-like grip around his prick was too much for Jeremy. His scrotum contracted hard and he fired a big wad of hot jism straight into the yummy mummy's colon. Another followed and then several more until he finally collapsed in a sweaty heap across her back.

When he had finally recovered enough, Jeremy peeled himself off his lover's back, kissing her on the cheek before he left her. "Fuck, that was good," he said to her before turning to Michelle. "Did you get it all?" he asked. He patted Monica on the bottom cheek before addressing her again. "We'll splice your footage with the film you saw earlier," he said. "We'll do this again.. and again," he added meaningfully.

Monica looked over her shoulder at him with passion burning in her eyes. She said nothing but the her acceptance and acquiescence was clear.

"Oh, my wife is going to love you," Jeremy chuckled.

PIMPING THE NEIGHBOUR'S WIFE

Jane had great fun fucking Penny, the adulterous neighbour's wife that her husband, Scott had blackmailed and entrapped. Their afternoon of unbridled passion next door had fuelled several weeks of passionate sex between the married couple as they recalled and re-enacted some of the hot and degrading action they had inflicted on the naive MILF and her toy boy. The boyfriend, David hadn't been seen since. He had run a mile once it was clear his dangerous liaison with his boss's wife was no longer a secret. Scott was still visiting Penny most afternoons but Jane wanted more. She had enjoyed dominating Penny so much she needed to do it again and much, much more. She wanted to up the ante and had a good idea how.

Lying in bed with her honey blonde hair spread across her husband's broad chest, she flicked through call girl ads on her tablet. "Oh, I can definitely see Penny in that get up," she chuckled, showing Scott the screen.

"Are you obsessed with getting the poor woman on the game," Scott answered. "That's a dangerous obsession and a dangerous game, full of even more dangerous people."

"Not necessarily," Jane replied. "Remember Kathryn, my old college friend?"

"I couldn't forget her!" She was the well-heeled, tall and sultry society type that gave Scott a hard on every time he thought about her.

"Prostitute!"

"No way! You're joking, right?"

"Nope! Kate spends a couple of evenings a week in a five star hotel and picks up about five grand for it. She spends the rest of her time doing whatever the hell she likes!"

"Don't you get any ideas," Scott chuckled.

"I've got lots of ideas," Jane came back." None of them involve me spreading my legs for rich fat men. Penny, however …!"

The following weekend, Jane lunched with Kathryn the call girl and hatched a plan. She then passed a message via Scott to Penny. She was taking her out that night and they would be back very late. Just so she could warn her husband off. The idea of not agreeing to come was not an option and both women knew it. The portfolio of film and stills the couple had on her would finish her marriage and probably her husband's business. She knocked on the door at seven o'clock, kissed the fragrant Penny on the cheek, waved to her unsuspecting husband and ushered the woman into her car.

"Where are we going?" Penny asked nervously as the MR2 pulled away.

"The Hilton. We're meeting some friends."

Penny knew Jane well enough by now to understand that 'meeting some friends' was code for 'some men she had never met before were going to fuck her.' She sat in silence for the rest of the short journey.

Jane picked up the key to her booked suite and the girls rode the lift together up to the top floor. A young couple got out half way up, leaving then alone. Jane turned the other woman towards her and had a good look at her. She was wearing a short fur coat on top of a little black dress with gold jewellery. She looked good and Jane's slight reservation that she might have to re-dress her for the role was dispelled. Even though Penny had no real idea what she was going to be doing, she was prepared perfectly. Her curvy body was showcased perfectly without being too cheap, her soft brown hair shone and fell around her shoulders and her make up was just right. She held her by the chin and kissed her intimately, slipping her tongue just inside her mouth. "I'm going to eat you like a banquet as soon as we get inside," she whispered.

The suite was amazing. The lounge area had a sunken sofa and surround sound cinema. There was a Jacuzzi and full bar and then there was the bedroom... "Wow! I've never seen such luxury before," Penny sighed.

Jane led her by the hand to the bed. "Lie back," she breathed. "I'm going to make love to you." Running her hand up the woman's soft inner thigh, she placed several soft kisses on her way to her ultimate goal. Peeling back the delicate gusset of her little red panties, Jane licked around the protruding lips of Penny's bald pussy, before sinking her long middle finger straight into her warm, moist insides.

Penny let out a little squeak as her Mistress penetrated her. Despite being a mother of one and having recently accommodated several large cocks, she still felt tight on being entered and even a finger always felt a little snug. Jane started a steady rhythm of licking around her slut's clitoris and pumping her cunt with her finger and maintained it for several minutes, until Penny's hips began to pump up and down and her moans telegraphed her impending orgasm.

Abruptly stopping and pulling out her finger, Jane kissed Penny on her full, ripe lips, letting her taste herself. "That'll do for now," she smiled. "You're ready. Now go and freshen up before our guests arrive."

When Penny came out of the bathroom, Jane held her hand out. "Your knickers please," she said. "You won't be needing them. Slip them off and relax on the bed."

As Penny made herself comfortable there was a soft knock at the door. "Here's your first guest," Jane told her. "Just you make sure you treat him well."

Jane opened the door to see a swarthy looking Arab in an expensive looking business suit. She ushered him in and offered him a drink. "Do you have the money?"

He produced a fistful of notes from his pocket with one hand and put his other on Jane's cheek. "It looks like you are worth every penny," he crooned.

"That's very flattering," Jane purred in reply. "But I'm not what you're paying for, let me show you." She took his hand and led the man into the bedroom, where Penny was propped up on the pillow. "For the next hour, she's all yours," she said. "You can do whatever you like to her as long as you don't cause any damage." With that, she kissed the man on the cheek and closed the door behind her.

Penny lay stock still on the bed, her heart pounding. She had heard every word spoken next door and realised this man was paying to have sex with her. She was a whore! She should have just got up and walked out but she couldn't. And it wasn't just because Jane had a hold over her with the pictures. It was something else entirely. She didn't want to!

The man was foreign, fit looking and not unattractive. He walked around the bed and stroked her soft brown hair. "You are a beautiful woman," he said in lightly accented but good English. "What is your name?"

"P-Penny," she stammered, without even thinking to give him a false one.

"An appropriate name," he laughed. "I am paying many pennies to have you. I am Ahmed and I would like to see you play with yourself, while I undress." Penny didn't think twice about it. She let her thighs drift open and moved her right hand down to her clitty, while squeezing her sensitive breasts through her dress with the other. Ahmed undressed and meticulously folded his clothes as he watched the English rose fuck herself for him. Her chest was already rising and falling heavily as her finger dipped inside her very moist vulva. When his underpants came off, her breath caught audibly in her throat. "Yes, I am big, no?" he laughed.

Big was quite possibly an understatement. Ahmed's cock had barely come to like but was already by far the biggest penny had ever seen. She tried to measure it in her mind and reckoned it must be twelve inches long and very fat. She had no idea if she could take it inside her little pussy but she knew she would have to try. Once completely naked, Ahmed crooked a finger and beckoned to the horny woman. "Crawl over here Penny!"

Turning over on to her hands and knees, Penny did exactly as commanded; quickly finding herself on eye level with his enormous trouser python. Without further direction, she reached for his cock and wrapped her little hand around it; at least almost around it. It was so thick, she couldn't make her fingers meet. She rubbed it a couple of times as if it were the genie's lamp and felt it throb in her hand. The power of the thing was just incredible and she actually felt intimidated by it.

"Put it in your mouth, little Penny," Ahmed commanded, encouraging her with a light touch on the back of her head. She opened her mouth as wide as she possibly could; so much she felt the skin stretch across her cheeks and dropped her head down to meet her hand.

Jane took a peep from the door and was staggered by the sight of Ahmed's cock. Penny was trying stoically to suck on the monster but there was no way she was going to close her moth over it. Instead, she settled for wanking him hard while sucking on the very tip and running her tongue along the underside.

Ahmed settled for that for a few minutes and then got bored. Rolling the horny housewife on to her back, he spread her thighs and positioned his meaty cock carefully against her slippery opening. With a grunt, he managed to wedge the end between her petals and began to slowly but surely open her up.

Penny's eyes widened at the same time as her pussy. She wriggled her bottom around as she became accustomed to the huge slab of man meat in her little twat. He pushed a little and she felt a jolt of pain and pleasure transmit itself through her pussy. And then he shoved. Hard! "Arrrgh!" Penny screamed out as her cunt suddenly opened to unimagined dimensions. It hurt a lot but the overall sensation was ecstasy. Pure ecstasy! She put her hands on the man's muscular shoulders and breathed in his exotic scent as he began slowly to hump her.

Penny's mind raced as the big, big man sent frissons of pleasure through her with each movement. She thought about her boring marriage and how she had tried to liven things up for herself with an affair. Then how her predatory neighbour had somehow found out about it and used the information to blackmail her into becoming little more than a sex toy for him and his wife. And now this! She had somehow become a prostitute. She was offering herself for money!

Ahmed's thrusts had increased in tempo and Penny's twat had somehow loosened enough to ease the movement. He squeezed her tits hard and used them to pull the horny wife on to his cock. Turning up the speed, his bare arse became a blur as he fucked her hard and fast until, finally, his balls contracted and he filled her womb with warm spunk. "Maybe we'll make a good Muslim baby together," he chuckled as he withdrew his softening cock from her with an audible pop.

Penny just lay there as Ahmed dressed. She felt used but oddly satisfied, even though she hadn't quite cum. He paused to kiss her on the cheek and then left the room, thanking Jane on the way past. Jane popped her head in the door. "Well done, sweetheart," she said kindly. "You've just earned three hundred quid. Go and clean up, you've got fifteen minutes until your next client."

The next customer was a lot different. Clint was American, rich and fat. And he had particular tastes. "Undress for me," he commanded as he heaved his bulk into an armchair near the bed. Jane had anticipated this and pressed the button on a CD player, filling the room with strains from The Stripper. Penny began to sway with the music and slowly reached behind her to unzip her dress and let it drop to the floor in a pool around her feet. Her panties were missing but she still wore her red satin bra. Doing her best to imitate what she imagined a real stripper would do, she rubbed her body along the fat man's thighs and offered up her big tits for him to grope. Reaching behind her back, she released the bra clasp and her ample bosoms fell right into Clint's face. He wasted no time in slobbering all over them and taking the nipples into his mouth.

Letting Penny's nipple drop from his mouth, Clint looked up at the sexy woman. "Take my cock out and blow me, slut," he said simply.

What a charmer! Penny thought as she did exactly as directed. His cock was predictably small; about the size of one of Ahmed's balls! She pulled it out with some difficulty and popped it into her mouth, sucking away at it until it was hard and an unimpressive four inches or so. Clint grabbed her head roughly and pumped into her mouth for a while before he decided he was ready for the main event. "Lie on your front," he commanded. "I'm gonna fuck your ass!"

Penny wasn't enamoured at the idea. She had taken a cock in her arse quite recently, thanks to Scott, her neighbour and it had hurt. The idea of having this fat man's excessive bulk hammering into her tight bottom was more than a little scary. He was at least using plenty of lubricant. As she rolled on to her front, he spread generous amounts of gel between her buttocks and up and down his shaft. Finally he was ready. Grunting with the effort, he climbed on to the bed and onto the backs of her thighs, crushing her into the bed. Carefully lining his cock up with her pretty little starfish, he pushed hard. Penny felt a little pressure and then he was in.

It hurt a little as Penny's sphincter gave in but nor too much. Her arse was inexperienced but the other cock she had taken there was much larger. Spreading her buttocks with his big meaty hands, Clint humped her as hard as he could. His weight crushed her into the mattress and big droplets of sweat rolled off his face and on to her back. Penny felt disgusted but also hotter than she could ever have imagined. The fat man reached underneath her and found her clitty with his sausage like fingers and it was as if he had lit her blue touch paper. Her whole body suddenly felt alive, her head span and her clitty buzzed. Suddenly her orgasm hit her like an express train. An electric feeling started in her clit and wound its way up her body and then her arse clamped hard around Clint's cock and she screamed out her pleasure. "Ohhh fuck!!"

Clint literally had the spunk milked out of him. He struggled to thrust into the constricted passage two or three more times and then couldn't handle it any more. He came with a strangled cry that sounded almost girl-like. Almost sheepishly, he tucked himself away and left without a word.

"How was that one?" It was Jane, leaning against the doorframe of the bedroom.

"More satisfying than I imagined," replied Penny, still lying on her front and regaining her equilibrium. "Have I finished?"

"Hardly," Jane laughed. "You have earned eight hundred quid though. Go and clean yourself up for the next clients."

"Clients? With an 's'?"

"You'll see!"

Penny was still in the shower when there was a loud knock on the door. Jane answered to find her clients; three young rugby players on a stag night. "Come on in fellahs," she smiled. "Who's the groom?"

"This is Ted," slurred a mountainous man, slapping his slightly shorter comrade on the back and propelling him into the room. "You ready for us darling?" Grabbing her round the waist, he pulled her towards him for a slobbery kiss.

"Easy tiger," Jane cried, good naturedly. "Your party's through there," she indicated the bedroom.

The other two put their head around the door. "Don't see anyone else," said the groom.

"Come on sweets," the bear of a man still holding her grunted. "No need to be shy." In one movement he pulled the front of her dress down and took one of her nipples into her mouth as his hand made its way through her skirt to find her pussy. In less than a minute, the protesting Jane had been bent over the table and her knickers were gone. Seconds later and the man was inside her.

When Penny came out of the en suite, she was staggered to see Jane on her hands and knees, being pushed backwards and forward by two hulking men. One was buried in her pussy while the other was jamming himself into her throat. "Hey! Looks like the party started without me," she laughed.

"Hey gorgeous, you playing too," asked the one of the three that was only watching.

"Sorry to disappoint stud," she laughed. "I'm the booker, not the hooker! Besides, I know for a fact that my friend here can take all three of you." She patted Jane on the arse; she was in no place to argue."

After taking a wad of notes off the young man, Penny stood aside while they manoeuvred a still protesting Jane around. The groom sat on an armchair with his impressive cock stood to attention and Jane was lifted and dropped straight on to it, squealing as it squeezed its way into her cunt. The biggest of the three men stood to the side of the chair and grabbed her head, to feed his cock into her open man. Finally the groom stood up on the edge of the chair and slowly worked himself into her arse. It took a couple of minutes but finally they all got there; Jane was airtight. With careful coordination, they timed their thrusts to work together and the helpless woman was heartily fucked in all three holes.

By the time the men had finished with her, Jane looked completely fucked. She could hardly move and had spunk dripping down her leg and chin. Penny kissed them and said goodbye before throwing her nemesis a towel. "I won't go so far as to say we're quits but it was nice to see you take the load for a change."

Jane lifted her head. "If that's an apology it's not necessary," she purred. "That was the best fucking I've had in a long time."

MILKING THE MILFS.

Professor Ed Dorking was ready to interview his new candidates. His prolific milker Diane had done really well to recruit six of her surrogate group for him and he had no doubt others would follow in due course. And the women themselves showed a great deal of potential, judging by their initial medical examinations. They had all been given a dose of his special formula and were sleeping off the initial effects while it silently went to work on their bodies.

The first interview was with Maureen and Wendy was conducting it with them. In fact, Ed had already divvied up the 'practicals' with his staff and Wendy had especially asked for this very special, big titted divorcee. The interview started in the conventional manner as Maureen was brought into a large office where Ed and Wendy were already sat. She was dressed in her street clothes again and Ed noted with a wry smile that the drug had already had a noticeable effect on her body. Her blouse was now straining to contain her very prominent bust; which seemed to have grown a couple of sizes. It must have been quite uncomfortable and he suspected she wouldn't take much talking out of her clothes.

Ed ran through the woman's details on the application form. Divorcee, no kids of her own, two-times surrogate, lives on her own, no current boyfriend, no regular job. Perfect! The thirty year old woman was a little plain but clear skinned, wide-eyed and had a special kind of innocence which was endearing. He began the questioning. "What you know about our work here, Maureen?"

"You're some sort of science institute and need women who are producing milk for your research," she began.

"Do you know how much we pay?"

"Erm, Diane said it's a lot!"

"We pay four thousand pounds a month with free accommodation and food," Ed replied.

"Wow!" Maureen was openly staggered.

"That is a lot of money and we expect a lot for it in return," Ed continued. "You're right, we do want your milk and the drug we have given you will enhance your yield; amongst other things." Ed continued and scrutinised the woman sat across from him. She was flushed and uncomfortable, her pulse was racing and her breasts were now throbbing. She needed attention soon but didn't yet realise. Ed had seen this stage many times in his subjects and had grown to love the challenge of moving them on. This time though, it was going to be Wendy breaking her in, he was just her assistant.

Wendy continued the conversation. "We do expect a lot," she said, getting up from her chair and moving behind the nervous woman. "In fact, for the time you are with us, we expect all of you." She laid her hands lightly on her shoulders. "How do you feel about that?" Maureen started to say something and then apparently felt better of it and shut her mouth again. Her head was spinning and she felt completely confused. The woman's close proximity was unsettling her and she didn't really know why. "Stand up," said Wendy sharply and the woman obeyed without question. Wendy lowered her hands slowly down Maureen's cleavage and began to unbutton her blouse. "It's time to test your milk for sweetness," she said, as if it were the most natural thing in the world.

Ed watched as his young protégée slowly massaged the older woman's huge mammaries as she removed her blouse. When her bra came off, his breath stuck in his throat. This woman was magnificent. Her big pink areolae were encircled by Wendy's small hands as she squeezed and manipulated them as she nuzzled at her neck. Turning Maureen around to face her, she lowered her head and took one of the long, erect nipples in her mouth without a word. The professor tried to read the woman's face as her barriers came crashing down. He was never really sure if the compliance of his subjects at this vital stage of their development was due to the inducement of riches or the drug enhanced hormones raging through their systems. Whichever it was, he had found the perfect storm and now Maureen, like all those horny women before her and many more yet to come, had crossed the Rubicon. There would be no return for her.

Wendy was slurping down warm sweet milk now and Maureen was in no fit state to stop her. On the contrary, she subconsciously arched her back to push her big boobs further into the younger woman's face. Wendy slipped her delicate hand down the voluptuous woman's abdomen and into the top of her panties, feeling the heat of her arousal. Moving her index finger through the thick curls, she brushed lightly along Maureen's exposed clitoris, causing her to grunt out loud. Finding that amusing, she stop sucking and looked the dark divorcee in the eyes as she deliberately speared her with two fingers.

"Oooh!" Maureen moaned as her legs almost buckled beneath her.

"So you like that slut?" Wendy asked, gripping her around the back of the neck with her left hand as she began to frig her hard with her right. The older woman was now putty in her hands and she intended to take full advantage of that. Removing her fingers, she first sniffed them herself and then held them up in front of Maureen's face. "Lick!"

Maureen didn't even hesitate before taking the young woman's sticky fingers into her mouth, enthusiastically licking her own juices off. Wendy waited until her hand was completely clean and then pushed down on the cooperative woman's shoulders; gently but firmly forcing her to her knees so she was face to twat with the professors assistant. Wendy hiked up her mid-thigh length dress and pushed her face into her gusset, rubbing herself off on Maureen's face. "Take my knickers down and eat me out you horny bitch," she moaned.

Maureen obediently peeled down Wendy's underwear and tentatively put out her tongue to taste the tangy juices. As she made contact with the moist slit, she jumped back as though her tongue had touched a battery terminal, Wendy sniggered and grabbed the woman's head again to smash her face against her soppy pussy. "Put your tongue in and eat me properly if you want to be fucked," you daft cunt," she moaned. Maureen's hands came up to tightly grip Wendy's firm buttocks as she brought her off.

Wendy enjoyed using the mature woman as a sex aid for a few more minutes before pulling her to her feet and bending her over the table. Ripping her knickers of with a strength that belied her slim physique, she slapped her hard on her naked arse. "Stay there. Don't move if you know what's good for you." Shuffling around in her bag, she produced a feldoe strapless dildo and fed it easily into her own moist pussy. Spreading the brunette's pear-shaped buttocks, she inserted the fat end and pushed. "Arrrgh!" Maureen cried out with passion and just a little discomfort as her vulva was opened up for the first time in many months.

As his favourite employee began to hump the newest member of his dairy herd, Ed left them to it. He had another interview conduct and would be doing this one alone. Closing the door on the increasing crescendo of sighs and moans, he moved next door to prepare to induct Milly; the teenager.

Milly was brought in to him and looked a little out of sorts. She had not been awake for long and looked like it, her pretty young face was bleary eyed, which only increased her look of vulnerability. Her slim and fragile body had changed a little in her sleep. Whereas she was almost flat-chested before she went to sleep, there was now a very obvious bulge in her tee shirt. Ed ran through the usual questions before hitting her with the special questions he had for her. "How many men have you slept with Milly? I mean had sex with?"

The nineteen year old was visibly shocked by the direct question and hesitated a little before stuttering her answer. "None!"

"None? Are you trying to tell me you're a virgin Milly? How does that work? You're a mother!"

"I was impregnated by syringe," the shy girl said quietly.

"You mean you've never had a man between your thighs? A hard cock spreading your tight pussy open. A man's tongue or finger strumming on your little clitty? A cock in your mouth or bottom?"

Milly flushed and began to breathe heavily. Ed could see she was clearly aroused; the effect of his words being magnified many times over by the drugs surging through her system. He continued. "Has anyone ever sucked your ripe little titties Milly?" He stood up and leant over her, intimidating her and adding to her confusion. "When did you last express?" he apparently changed tack.

Milly checked her watch. "About six hours ago," she said.

"Ow!" Ed said sympathetically. "Are they full and tender?" Without asking he squeezed her little round breasts through her tee shirt.

"Ow!" Milly repeated.

Without asking permission, Ed raised the girl's tee shirt and she compliantly raised her arms so he could remove it. Reaching around her as though holding her in an embrace, he deftly unfastened her bra and slipped it off to gaze appreciatively at her firm, apple-shaped tits and succulent, cherry red nipples. She had flushed from the points of those nipples, all the way to the roots of her silky red hair. Ed tore his eyes away from the girl's bosom and looked deep into her green eyes. He saw confusion, passion and compliance. With a guiding hand on her slim back, he dropped his head and sucked one of Milly's delicious little nubs into his mouth and sucked hard until he received a steady flow of sweet milk.

Milly sat dead still on her chair as Ed suckled on first one tit and then the other. Her nipples were rock hard and her whole body tingled with desire. Gently fondling her, he let the nipple slip from his mouth and spoke softly to her, with his face only inches from her own, his breath warm on her cheek. "You taste delicious my dear. How does that feel?"

"It feels odd," Milly replied honestly, "but very, very good!"

"Good," Ed replied, tipping the girl's head back with his fingers on her chin and covering her open mouth with his own. As he explored her sweet mouth with his tongue, his hands ran freely over her firm body, stroking her soft skin and pulling on her swollen nipples. Without unlatching his mouth from hers, he slowly pulled her to her feet and unbuttoned her jeans, forcing the unyielding material down her thighs. Milly's white cotton knickers were stretched tightly over her prominent mound and as Ed's fingers found her, she jumped as though she'd received an electric shock. Her panties soon followed her jeans and Ed finally stopped snogging the horny girl to pull both garments off her feet with her shoes and spinning her around to bend her over the interview table. "Stay in that position," he whispered, punctuating his command by slipping his middle finger into her very moist and very tight pussy. He then had second thoughts, span her around and lifted her on to the table, to let her fall back on to her back. It wasn't often he had the opportunity to fuck a virgin and he wanted to watch every moment of her deflowering replayed in her eyes. Sucking the milk out of her tits again, he pushed his finger back into her.

After fingering the helpless girl several times, to leave her whimpering with passion, Ed removed his own trousers and underwear before seizing her firmly by her slim hips and pulling her back towards her. "I'm going to fuck you now my dear," he told her. "You should know that I'm quite well built and you are evidentially very small so we're going to have to work together to make it a pleasurable experience for you."

"Please don't hurt me," the teenager whimpered.

Ed gently pushed so that just the very tip of his dick entered her. Even with less than a half inch inside, Milly's pussy lips seemed to be stretched tight around him, which felt really good. As he continued to penetrate her, her eyes widened and he became aware she was panting hard as though in labour and then, as his big helmet popped through the muscle ring, she began to whine like a dog. The further he entered, the better it felt. Milly was wrapped around him so tightly, she seemed grafted to his manhood.

Eventually Ed bottomed out with at least two inches of his cock still outside the tiny pussy. As his flesh pressed against Milly's cervix, she let out a long, tortured cry of passion. "Oooooh!" Tightening his grasp on her hips, he pulled out of her, nearly turning her cunt inside out in the process and then slammed back in hard enough to shoot her out of his own grip so that her pelvis smashed against the edge of the table. "Oh God that's so good!" Milly cried out in answer to his efforts.

There was no way Ed was going to last long in this tight, fragrant virgin. Her vulva seemed to be milking his cock every time he pulled out and he could feel his balls tighten. He was determined to give the horny little slut her orgasm first though, to make her first fucking truly memorable. Looking deep into her eyes, he cradled her head in his hand and changed his rhythm to hump her with little rabbit strokes. With the change in tempo, the angle of penetration also altered and Milly felt his thick, nobbly shaft brush along her g spot, creating an electrical effect. Milly thought her head was going to explode. With the delightful buzzing starting in her groin, the friction in her love tunnel and the wonderful throbbing of her boobs, she quickly succumbed. Her pussy started to convulse and suddenly Ed's big cock pulsed and spat out its load of baby batter; deep inside her. The thought of being impregnated in this way was too much for Milly and her cunt just exploded. Her body bucked, her head swam and she literally screamed, "Arrrrgh!"

Ed pulled out of the teenager with some difficulty, leaving a string of jism between them. Patting her affectionately on the bottom, he zipped himself up. "You'll fit in just fine around here Milly," he said. "Just you stay there for a few minutes and someone will come and collect you." He ruffled her red hair affectionately and left the room. She'd be taken back to her room and cleaned up before being taken down to the milking room. He grabbed a beer from the fridge in his office and flicked on his CCTV monitor. Incredibly Wendy was still going on Maureen. The older woman was on her knees with her arms tied behind her back to thrust her huge breasts out and upwards. Wendy was holding her by the head and thrusting her strapless dildo down the woman's throat. Her tits were bouncing with each entry and Ed could just make out the drool running out of the corner of her mouth. He would have to rescue her soon or she'd be worn out, he thought wryly. He never realised Wendy had so much energy. He would have to find an outlet for that. He flicked across to the other rooms. Cat and Doreen were already being fucked and Helen was sat at the interview table with his assistants John and Mel. He had a good look at Cat's initiation. She was sat down on Eric's considerable cock, while Mark held her head and fed her his own slim penis and Kirk crouched behind her and held her firmly by the hip as he tried to get his own tool into her arse. Finally, a long squeal from the elegant brunette revealed his success and Ed marvelled at the first triple initiation. He finished his beer and prepared mentally for the last interview – stroppy Miss Katie.

This interview and initiation was going to be conducted by four of them, three strong men and a very lesbian woman; Tilly. Katie was not a typical subject. Thirty five years old, she looked more like a company executive than a surrogate mother and had the attitude to match. She had rebelled during her inspection and several times since and Ed knew she was going to be trouble. All the same, he couldn't resist a challenge. Sure enough, when he asked her to stand up and remove her top, she refused. "You must be joking. What do you think this is?"

"I'm offering you a great deal of money for your milk, young lady," Ed lectured her. "If you want to be a part of my team, you need to learn to do things my way."

"I'm not a prostitute," the attractive blonde huffed. "If you want my milk, I will express it in private."

"Really!" Ed laughed and nodded to James and Mike. The two amateur bodybuilders grabbed an arm each and held her firmly while Tilly slowly unbuttoned her expensive blouse, looking meaningfully into her eyes. Her bra came next and the butch dyke lifted her shapely breast to her face, sniffed her scent and then popped the nipple into her mouth. "This is our preferred method of milking here," Ed continued to instruct the rebellious woman, who was struggling as much as she could to no avail but now curiously quiet. He walked across and held her pretty face by the chin, between his finger and thumb and looked straight into her eyes. "I'm going to teach you who's in charge here Katie and then I'm going to fuck you; hard!" He dropped his head and sucked on her free tit.

By the time Ed and Tilly had emptied the woman's milk ducts, she was already largely compliant as her hormones had taken control. All the same, he wanted to be sure she had the message, loud and clear. He stepped clear and the other two men bent her across the desk, Mike holding her wrist firmly from the other side as James ripped down her trousers and panties. Removing his belt, Ed gave her a good twelve strokes before allowing James the first fuck. Raising her tear stained face, she looked completely lost in pain, confusion and complete lust and she yelled with passion as he entered her. Once James had finished, it was Mike's turn for sloppy seconds and there was no longer any need for her to be restrained. She bucked with lust, not resistance.

When Mike had emptied his balls into the blonde's overflowing cunt, Ed lifted her off the table and Tilly hopped up, already stripped from the waist down. Ed pushed Katie back over and encouraged her face into the dyke's minge. There was no fight back. The straight, professional woman grabbed Tilly's buttocks and slurped away at her pussy juices like a life-long lesbian. One final taboo remained. Squeezing some lube on to his fingers from a tube in his pocket, Ed slid them into Katie's tight arsehole.

Unzipping himself, he lined up with her rosebud and pushed, breaking through her sphincter in one go. She moaned into Tilly but didn't resist; merely upping her rate of lapping. Ed slapped her firm arse and buggered her relentlessly. Another worthy addition to his herd was ready for exploitation.

ABOUT THE AUTHOR

A suburban Mum by day and who likes to let her hair down at night. Either blessed or cursed with a high sex drive, Charlotte is lucky to have a fantastic husband who looks after her in every respect but also allows her to research all aspects of her writing. She loves to write about sexy submissive ladies because at heart that's what she is. She writes about her girls being put into often extreme and difficult circumstances by strong men who care about them and ultimately ensure they are loved and looked after. She writes what she likes to read and it appeals to men and women alike.

Printed in Great Britain
by Amazon

75676113R10037